Parents and Caregivers,

Stone Arch Readers are designed to provide enjoyable reading experiences, as well as opportunities to develop vocabulary, literacy skills, and comprehension. Here are a few ways to support your beginning reader:

- Talk with your child about the ideas addressed in the story.

- Discuss each illustration, mentioning the characters, where they are, and what they are doing.

- Read with expression, pointing to each word. You may want to read the whole story through and then revisit parts of the story to ensure that the meanings of words or phrases are understood.

- Talk about why the character did what he or she did and what your child would do in that situation.

- Help your child connect with characters and events in the story.

Remember, reading with your child should be fun, not forced. Each moment spent reading with your child is a priceless investment in his or her literacy life.

Gail Saunders-Smith, Ph.D.

STONE ARCH READERS

are published by Stone Arch Books
A Capstone Imprint
1710 Roe Crest Drive
North Mankato, Minnesota 56003
www.capstonepub.com

Library of Congress Cataloging-in-Publication Data
  Meister, Cari.
  The clever dolphin / by Cari Meister ; illustrated by Steve Harpster.
  p. cm. — (Stone Arch readers—ocean tales)
  Summary: Piper is trapped in a tuna net and it is up to Meko the dolphin to rescue her sister.
  ISBN 978-1-4342-4027-9 (library binding) — ISBN 978-1-4342-4229-7 (pbk.)
  1. Dolphins—Juvenile fiction. 2. Sisters—Juvenile fiction. 3. Rescues—Juvenile fiction. [1. Dolphins—Fiction. 2. Sisters—Fiction. 3. Rescues—Fiction.] I. Harpster, Steve, ill. II. Title.

PZ7.M515916Cle 2012
[E]—dc23

2011050081

Art Director: Kay Fraser
Designer: Russell Griesmer
Production Specialist: Kathy McColley

Reading Consultants:

Gail Saunders-Smith, Ph.D.
Melinda Melton Crow, M.Ed.
Laurie K. Holland, Media Specialist

Printed in China
032012   006677RRDF12

The Clever DOLPHIN

by Cari Meister

illustrated by Steve Harpster

STONE ARCH BOOKS
a capstone imprint

MEKO THE DOLPHIN

DOLPHIN FUN FACTS

- When dolphins sleep, half of their brains stay fully awake. This keeps them aware of dangers.

- Dolphins are able to swim up to 25 miles per hour, but they usually swim 7 to 8 miles per hour.

- The orca, also known as the killer whale, is actually a type of dolphin.

- Pink dolphins live in the Amazon River in South America.

Meko jumped in the air.

"I can't wait for tonight," she clicked.

"Do you think I will be picked to be the new scout?" she asked her little sister, Piper.

Scouts helped keep the pod safe. They also found food for everyone.

"You are the fastest dolphin," said Piper.

"And the highest jumper!" added Meko.

Meko swam swiftly along the waves. Piper tried to keep up. But Meko was too fast.

Meko jumped again. When she splashed down, she knew something was wrong.

Piper was not there!

"Piper!" clicked Meko. "Where are you?"

Piper did not click back. Meko dived under the waves. She saw a school of tuna, but no Piper.

Meko came up for a breath.
She looked out over the ocean.

She saw a fishing boat, but no Piper.

"Piper!" she clicked. "Where are you?"

Meko swam home. She was scared.

"What's wrong?" asked her dad.

"Where is Piper?" asked her mom.

Meko fell to the ocean floor.
She moaned.

"I don't know," she cried. "I
looked everywhere."

Meko's little sister was gone!
Lost! Or worse, eaten!

"It's all my fault!" said Meko.
"If I wasn't showing off, I would
have seen where Piper went!"

"Did you see an orca?" asked her mom. Orcas often ate dolphins.

"No," said Meko.

"Did you see a school of hammerhead sharks?" asked her dad. Hammerheads ate dolphins, too.

"No," said Meko.

They relaxed a little. "Let's
form a search party," said her
dad. "Maybe she just wandered
away and got lost."

A group of dolphins swam
west. They jumped and raced.

Another group of dolphins
swam east. They clicked and
chirped and whistled for Piper.

Meko was still on the ocean
floor. "There must be a clue,"
she said. "Let me think."

Meko flapped a flipper. "I know!" she said. She raced back to where she saw the boat. It was still there!

There were thousands of tuna
swimming around the boat.

"It's a tuna boat!" said Meko.
"There must be a tuna net
around here," she said.

Meko swam around to the
other side. She spotted her sister.

"Piper!" she clicked.

But Piper could not click back. Her nose was stuck in the net. She was trapped!

Meko clicked for the others.
They were too far away to hear.

It was up to Meko. She
grabbed the net and started
chewing and chewing. Soon
Piper was free!

That night, the scout leader held a meeting.

"I pick Meko as our new scout," he said. "Everyone knows that Meko is fast. Today she showed us that she is clever, too!"

Everyone shouted, "Way to go, Meko!"

The End

STORY WORDS

dolpin

moaned

fault

orca

relaxed

whistled

clever

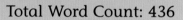

Total Word Count: 436

WHO ELSE IS SWIMMING IN THE OCEAN?

STONE ARCH READERS · LEVEL 3
The **Lucky** MANATEE
by Cari Meister
Illustrated by Steve Harpster

STONE ARCH READERS · LEVEL 3
The **Stranded** ORCA
by Cari Meister
Illustrated by Steve Harpster

STONE ARCH READERS · LEVEL 3
The **Grumpy** LOBSTER
by Cari Meister
Illustrated by Steve Harpster